Death From a Height

Armando Amarosa was quite the ladies' man. He was tall, good-looking, rich, had all the perfect lines, a very high-paying job, a large luxurious house, a yacht, a Maserati – what more could a man want?

So why did he jump from the tower? It was a place he took many a lady to watch the often spectacular sunrises and sunsets. His den room was filled with photos of a lovely lady with a colorful cloud formation behind.

Lt. Flores couldn't figure it. Why did so many of these people who had the world in the palm of their hand commit suicide?

Then the photos. Photos that Amarosa didn't take!

Contents

About the author

CD Moulton has traveled extensively over much of the world both in the music business, where he was a rock guitarist, songwriter and arranger and in an import/export business. He has been everything from a bar owner to auto salvage (junkyard) manager, longshoreman to high steel worker, orchid grower to landscaper, tropical fish farmer to commercial fisherman. He started writing books in 1983 and has published more than 350 books as of January 1, 2023. His most popular books to date are about research with orchids, though much of his science fiction and fantasy work has proven popular. He wrote the CD Grimes, PI series, and the Det. Nick Storie series, Clint Faraday series, and many other works.

He now resides in Gualaca, Chiriqui, Panamá, where he writes books, plays music with friends, does research with orchids and medicinal plants. He has lately become involved in fighting for the rights of the indigenous people, who arc among his closest friends, and in fighting the extreme corruption in the courts and police in Panamá.

He offers the free e-book, *Fading Paradise*, that explains what he has been through because of the corruption.

CD is the discoverer of the Chadam Protocol for curing cancer.

Facebook page Ambrosia peruviana for cancer.

Death From a Height

<u>*The Good Life*</u>

Armando Antonio Amarosa looked into the mirror with a critical eye.

The suit would not do, tonight. Tonight was the kind of night he wanted a much more casual look.

Sylvia Morales was looking for excitement, so wouldn't care for the Ciudad de David or the Mosto Bistro. Maybe even Las Brasas was just a bit too upscale for this.

He would dress down, and take her to La Tipica. She could mingle with the "common people" and still enjoy very good food. It would be a lark. They could go from there to a local place of her choice. He was expert at choosing just the right outfit to match the psychology of the place he would take her. This would be a (designer) blue jean night. His line would be that she was over-dressed, that he was getting tired of taking a beautiful woman to a fancy place where the snobs hung out. She was much to good for that, but she had to fit for a truly fun night.

She wouldn't have a thing she could really dress

down in, but she wouldn't know that. Maybe she would use the Armantine thing, which was a drab cheap three hundred dollar outfit she wore when she went slumming. Estelline and Gucci and Florentine would be overdoing it. Maybe the plain black purse with the pearls. The emerald and diamond thing would be out of place.

Armando Antonio Amarosa knew how women thought. She would picture herself slumming in anything that cost less than a thousand dollars. It would still be the best thing at whatever place he took her. Those people probably didn't even own a dress that costs more than a hundred dollars. She would never accept that they probably didn't have a dress that costs more than twenty dollars.

Blue jeans, and one of those stylish tee shirts would do it. A cheap watch, and no jewelry. He would have to impress on her that one didn't wear a fifty thousand dollar necklace when she was slumming.

That wasn't fair. She didn't wear much jewelry, but she would have an expensive watch. It would be another thing where she didn't have anything that cost less than a thousand or so.

He slipped into the clothes of choice, and looked in the mirror again.

Not that slick hair! Bad choice.

He could rinse the spray out, and have a more

wild, casual look.

A few minutes later, as he left, he looked over his image in the full-length mirror on the bathroom door. He didn't like to sound vain, even to himself, but he really was a goodlooking dude!

That would be the type expression to use around the places he would go tonight.

He was just getting into his Maserati when he thought better of it. Show up slumming in a two hundred thousand dollar car! Just brilliant!

He went to the road, and flagged a taxi. That would be an experience for Sylvia Morales! A taxi! What would they think of next!

He felt good about tonight! He was going to get laid, which wasn't anything unusual, but it was going to be Sylvia Morales! A real prize! She was the ice queen, because she was hot and sexy and rich, and knew men were more after her money than anything else, other than a quickie.

Armando Antonio Amarosa was going to grab the big brass ring tonight, only it was the solid platinum ring! It was the prize everyone was after, but he was going to claim it!

He remembered when he went for the sex bit because he liked the sex bit. When did it come to the point where money figured into it? He had more now than was reasonable.

Maybe it was because these money women

didn't trust anyone who didn't have as much. They could figure he wasn't after money.

He wasn't. He was after the score card. He wanted to score more and better than anyone else. To be honest about it, he really didn't want to lay a lot of the ones he did. Sick, but it was better than total boredom.

Ah! The yacht. He'd take her out to the yacht. That would be more luxurious than any hotel.

He could figure on two o'clock AM, on the yacht. He liked to have these things scheduled, to see if he could stay on that schedule. So far, he'd come very close.

Sylvia Morales looked at herself in the mirror. Armando wanted to go slumming. He was male, so also wanted to show her off. His showroom girlfriend. He would expect her to overdress a lot for the night, then would take her to the better common places to show her off.

She was goodlooking. She'd spent a lot of money to be a knockout, and had dieted and exercised and worked to stay that way.

So Army was going to play the game he played with Gina and Sara and Betty and Gloria and Magali and who knew who else. She would get a real kick out of making him the prize, and her the winner.

She looked at the plain white blouse and tight skirt she'd bought at Poderoso for a total of nine dollars. She would wear the cheap blue sneakers. They were one hell of a lot more comfortable than those designer shoes that were designed to induce torture. She would look shapeless in that floppy blouse.

She was a knockout, and knew it. He would depend on her wanting to show off her "assets," as they called it. He would be dressed to look like the superstud he pictured himself as being. He was goodlooking, and kept in excellent shape. He probably was good in bed, unlike so many who were goodlooking, and thought that was all it took.

She took the cheap silver and turquoise bracelet she'd bought from a street vendor. She really did like it, and it would fit in with this outfit. She'd learned, a long time ago, that some of the cheaper things were far more attractive than the expensive overdone things.

What could she do about her hair? It cost a hundred fifty for the do that was way too much for tonight.

She looked at her six wigs, and took the simple page-boy one to mess up a little. She used spray to make it less page-boy, got an idea, and made it look like some of the styles the people she would be around got.

She looked in the mirror again, and grinned. It was perfect! She would look like everyone else, but was still better looking than most.

The houseman came to say there was a ... person at the door to see her. He stared at what he was seeing.

"We're going slumming. He didn't bring that Maserati, did he? He would be the type to dress down to street level, then drive up in something like that."

Hanson grinned. "He must have thought of that bit. He has a taxi waiting."

She laughed, and slapped palms. Hanson was a buddy. He would truly enjoy this one! He had remarked about a couple of the guys she dated, saying they were incapable of enjoying life. He'd often said that she would have more fun with the regular people. She would have to drop the snob act.

She'd found that was true.

Essy (Estelle) Generoso looked in the mirror, and made a grimace. Still overdone.

Syl had told her about going slumming tonight with Army. She'd gone out with Army a couple of times, and found him to be shallow and a pig who only wanted sex. It seemed to be some kind of scorecard thing with him.

So she got emotionally involved, and got hurt. He wasn't the only one who did that to her. He'd played her for a fool, now Syl was going to play him for a fool. She had to see that!

The phone buzzed for a text message. She looked at it. La Tipica.

"Thanks, Syl! I'll happen to drop by. Let's see how he handles this one!"

She took another look at the mirror. She had time. She would manage to look like he probably thought Syl would look like. Syl would get a real kick out of that!

Amanda (Mandy, of course) Winters got the message, "La Tipica," on her text message, and grinned. She was the one who, as Syl said she was going to do tonight, went slumming. She hated dressing up. It just wasn't her.

Army was pulling that line on her. He'd show her off.

She knew that. She was going to look so much like a regular girl it would make you puke. The one who always looked like that was going to be the super class model of ostentation tonight.

La Tipica. She would have to contrive something that would explain her being there. It was really good food, and they knew her, a little, because she did go in, once in awhile.

Army. The slick line, he lays you, then he's out looking for someone else to use another line on.

She smirked at the mirror, and headed for the door. She knew how she would work it. Lover-boy superstud Army was going to find this night to be like a lot of nights he caused for other naive girls who found out a day late that she was just another number on a scorecard.

Sandra Bellows read the message. La Tipica.

She knew the place, because she drove by it, several times. It was popular, and the food was supposed to be very good.

She didn't go to those kinds of places. Ever. No maitre de, no Sandra Bellows.

Syl was getting Army there to do something. She was a lot more experienced with men than Sandra or most others in their strata. It would be, at least, spectacular, knowing Syl!

Should she break the rule, and go there? She would certainly enjoy seeing that slimy lying bastard son of a bitch taken down a few notches! If anyone could do that, Syl could!

Why were men such pigs? Why couldn't they be honest enough to say they wanted to screw, and not that they thought they were falling in love!

"What's love got to do with it?" by Tina Turner. How very damned disgustingly true!

"Well, Army, *dearest*, I hope you get it in the ass tonight. I can't think of a more deserving person – if you could call your kind of animal a person!

"Come to think of it, as handsome as you are, you might like it in the ass. It would explain how you can be so cruel and thoughtless with us girls!

"That's not really true. Kenny and Sam are gay, and they're wonderful to us. You're just a pig!"

She decided what she would do. She really did want to see Army taken down.

Gloria Sanchez saw the message, and an evil smirk crossed her pretty face. She would enjoy being part of this. Syl was a genius with this kind of thing. She outclassed Army, all the way. It was going to be a double slap to dear Army. He was going down, big time!

She was going to be there to see it. She and several of the conquests would be there to be a part of it.

This might even be great fun! She was over the hijo de puta. All the way.

The tight sexy split red Tango outfit. She was going to see that every guy and girl there noticed when dear Army got his come-uppance! Make yourself the center of attention, and be in the right spot at the right time!

This would be fun!

Syl said there were ten of the girls who had good reason to want to see that lousy damned bastard humiliated. She wondered who the others were. She could guess four or five of them.

Army didn't feel quite so confident as he paid the cab at La Tipica. Sylvia knew how to dress for slumming, which he hadn't counted on. It was going to be hard to show off his trophy when she was wearing that cheap stuff from some rack in a store on the strip.

He was glad he hadn't told any of his friends about this. He would play the game, get laid, and go home early.

Was that Mandy Winters getting out of a cab? He didn't even know she ever went to places like this – but she did go slumming. She'd told him that. Maybe this wasn't a good line to use. He really didn't do much slumming, himself.

He went in, and started for a table to the side, by the rail. Stay out of sight.

Damn it to hell! Sylvia plopped down at a table right in the middle of the place!

Make the best of it. Everyone who counted knew that Sylvia was the prize catch in David!

The waitress came. Sylvia said she'd heard the

camarones apanada here were the best, so ordered that. Army mumbled that it sounded good to him, too.

My God! Essy Generoso is coming in from the front? Does everyone I know come here? This was a big mistake!

"Well, where shall we go after here? I've heard there's a disco the locals like across from the Super Ninety Nine," Sylvia suggested.

"Er, um. We can try it. I don't really know this scene. It's just something that's different, so I wanted to find someone who's the best looking anywhere and who knows how to, er, fit."

"Oh, all us girls like to do this kind of thing, once in awhile. We'll meet some bad-ass bikers or something and fantasize about getting laid by a real stud. When it doeds happen, they're a big disappointment. They always think they're the superstud who women can't resist and ... perform like a self-indulgent jerk. Our crowd was raised different. We can never fit, but it's fun – if you don't take yourself too seriously."

"You go out to get laid?"

"Certainly! Isn't that why you go out?"

"I mean... I thought you were looking for a more solid, lasting thing."

"Sometimes, but we like to have a little fun, too.

"Oh! There's Gloria! I haven't seen her in

months! Gloria! Hi!"

Oh, shit! Now we get the fiery Latina! Shit!

"Hi, Syl! What? You're slumming tonight?"

"Yeah! Great fun. We're going over to that new disco. Want to come along?"

"Yeah! It'll be fun! Army can see what a real superstud looks and acts like!"

"Yeah! And they're almost always a big let-down!"

"Uh-huh! *Almost* always. Giggle giggle wink wink.

"Oh! That's Essy! Hi, Essy! How are tricks? Turned any lately?"

"I wish. I'm going to try out that new disco. Something about a frog, or something. Janet picked up that guy she's as much as moving into her place. She says he's the best fuck she ever had. She's used up everyone in our crowd, and says they're a bunch of amateurs.

"I'm just terrible! I shouldn't say such things where Army can hear, but it is true that our crowd isn't exactly known for satisfying a girl.

"Sorry, Army. Facts are facts."

A chauffeured Rolls Royce pulled up. A very attractive woman, wearing what had to be half a million dollars worth of jewels, got out.

"Syl! Gloria! I was going by, and saw you. I haven't seen you in *ages*, and wanted to say hello!

"I believe we've met? At the inauguration thing? You're Estelle Generoso, I believe. I'm Sandra Bellows. Just Sandy.

"I was just riding around, trying to find something that's not so damned boring to do.

"Hello, Armando. How have you been?

"Anyway, what's the party?"

"We just ran together here. We're going to try the new disco. We all have to take taxis, or we can walk. It's not far. Hint! Hint!" Sylvia said.

"Perfect! We can go in my car! I haven't been in that kind of place in five years! It'll be fun!"

The women started chatting and joking. Army was as much as left out. He was glad he got a phone call. He would make an excuse to leave. This bunch could go to the disco without him!

"Armando? I'm Donna Bergstrom. We met at that place where I was doing the modeling shoot for the Boutique group? You said to call you if I'm ever at loose ends. I'm in David, and am at loose ends."

Army thought, and remembered. He did meet her. She was a very attractive woman. If he could think of a way....

"Oh, Army! Let's finish this and go to the disco. I think it'll be great fun!" Sylvia suggested.

Damn! What a time to be with her! I can't make excuses!

"I'm afraid tonight's not good. I'll call you tomorrow, and we can find some diversion, I'm sure!"

"You have my number?"

"It's on the caller ID. I'll mark it. Very easy!"

He soon rang off. Everyone was bubbling about the disco. They finished their breaded shrimp. Army couldn't contrive to get away. He felt imprisoned. He'd slept with all but Sylvia here! He couldn't get away from this group! Tonight was a disaster in progress! They probably didn't even realize it, but they were cutting him down and chopping him up with everything they said.

They crowded into the Rolls, and were soon at the disco. They managed to get two tables to push together.

The conversation was embarrassing as hell to Army! All these women were talking about guys they knew, or some guy who was there and kept comparing them to "Our crowd," always with anyone but "Our crowd" really great in bed.

An hour of hell later, Sylvia told him she could see he wasn't having a good time. She would understand if he wanted to leave. If he saw a girl he liked there, feel free to lay a line on her. Tonight was going to turn into a night with the girls. She could see that, clearly enough!

A minute later, his phone rang again. He was

almost excited, thinking it might be Donna again.

"Army? This is Clara Enders. I saw you come in, and don't know how you can stand sitting there with that bunch of too-rich snobs. If you can get away, I would like to go to a quieter place."

Sylvia was looking at him. He grinned, and said he had a woman friend who wanted him to go to another place. He didn't really like this kind of noisy bar. Would she understand?

"Silly! I just said to go have some fun! Bye! Hope you get lucky!"

He sighed in relief, and went out.

Clara Enders wasn't a knockout beauty, and she wasn't rich. She was a very nice person. He had a better time with her, but she wouldn't go to bed the first date.

"We can meet tomorrow night. It will be the second date?" she suggested.

He said he knew the perfect place to start the evening. He would pick her up at six, so they could be there for the show.

"I don't generally care for shows. I think they're too phony."

"This is nature's show! I promise you'll like this one!"

She agreed to meet him tomorrow at six.

Army stood close, next to Clara. He couldn't understand why he was so attracted to her. She really wasn't his type.

The sunset, as he'd hoped, was spectacular. All salmons and pinks, with a little rose. They were on the observation tower at the old church. It was almost dizzying to watch those clouds as the colors slowly shifted. Hypnotic.

"I have to agree. This is quite a show. It's totally beautiful, suggesting fire and violence and tranquility, at the same time. Perhaps because the more violent darker colors are so far away. The mountain peak is a silhouette from a fantasy world.

"This is real. There's nothing phony about it, like in those silly picture shows I was afraid you would take me to."

"It's a warm place, with a warm feeling about it for a person I feel is a very warm person," Army replied. "The colors are perfect, tonight. They're moving people closer. Some nights, they move people apart.

"I can't express it. Last night, I should have

known would be a disaster. The colors were more into the red, and the formations were twisted and unpleasant. The morning was fantastic, but sunrises from here can be as beautiful, or moreso, than sunsets.

"I would have missed tonight if I hadn't been there, so it worked out very much for the best."

She leaned a bit tighter against him. "I feel tonight will be wonderful, myself!"

He moved to put an arm around her waist.

Lt. Renaldo "Naldo" Flores shook his head, and sighed. He saw the squad was taking all the necessary pictures, but this one almost had to be suicide.

It wasn't the first, here. Devout Catholics doing a swan dive to hell. Suicide was a mortal sin, yet they came to the old church tower to suicide.

Father Geraldo had come, just after daylight, to police the grounds under the tower, as always, and had found a man's body there. He had, apparently, jumped off the tower, and had hit on his back and slightly to the left. He didn't do the swan dive bit. He just climbed over the rail and dropped to the brick walk, sixty feet below.

"Time of death, tentatively, forty five minutes to an hour and a quarter ago. Five forty five to seven AM," Doc. Mendez said. "I'll get it closer at the morgue. I'd say six ten, as a guess.

"If I'm all that was needed, you can transport. I've seen what there is to see, here."

Naldo nodded, and looked around. It didn't feel right, somehow.

"Doc, can I say this is suicide? Could it be an accident?"

"That might be more likely. He hit on his back, which a suicide almost never would. If he sat on the rail, he might have fallen on his back."

"Would the rail stand his weight? That's an old tower. Two hundred years."

"It's been repaired. Two inch galvanized steel pipe. It would hold the weight."

"Did you find ID?"

"Yes. Armando Amarosa. I saw that, from the first. He was a very wealthy playboy, with a yacht and big luxury house at Boca Chica, and another estate up toward Dolega.

"You can go to the estate house, here. There might be something to find, and you'll have to tell whoever's there he won't be coming back."

Naldo nodded, again. He finished his crime scene review, and wrote the report that this was most probably an accidental death. The only question would be what he was doing on that tower after midnight.

Next would be to inform the family. He went to

the morgue to get the personal effects. There was no one listed to contact in case of accident or emergency.

He called the number of the house, but there was no answer, there. The machine said to leave a message.

Nothing to do but go to the house.

He found another number with BC before it. He called, and a woman answered who said she was the housekeeper, and that Mr. Amaroso would be in the Dolega house for the remainder of the month.

He told the crew he would be gone for awhile. Lt. Maria Lanias would accompany him to the house of the dead man. He got the keys from Doc. There were keys to a Maserati, there.

Naldo and Maria drove into the estate to find a Maserati sitting on the drive. They went to the door, but got no answer, so Naldo tried the keys. They went in, to find as luxurious a place as Naldo had ever seen. An old man and woman came in from the back. They explained that there was an alarm if the door was opened. They would go on duty at ten until seven thirty. They were the Carters, Amarosa's house staff.

"Did Mr. Amarosa often leave and not take that car out there?" Maria asked.

"Yes. When he was going to anyplace that had

no valet parking, he would take a taxi or go with a friend. He said that a car worth what the average person made in ten years was not a good item to have sitting on a street, somewhere."

"May I inquire as to why the police are here with the keys the Mr. carried? Is he in some kind of trouble?"

"No," Naldo replied. "I'm sorry to have to tell you, he is dead."

"Dead?"

"I think he had an accident, and fell a long distance."

"Fell? He ... was he taking photos at the tower, and fell? He knows it very well. It does not seem as likely he fell from there."

"He took a lot of photos from the tower?" Maria asked.

"Yes. He liked to photograph the sunrises and sunsets from there. He often took his lady friends up there to photograph them with the colors as background. There are many photos in his study. He also took the sunsets at Boca Chica, but those photographs are mostly in his study there."

"We will need to see some things here," Naldo said.

"Was he depressed, lately, for any reason?" Maria asked.

"Depressed? No. Quite to the contrary. He said

his life was charmed. He had everything in life a man could ask. He did not kill himself, officer."

They went into the large study. It was rich and comfortable. There were hundreds of photos of sunsets and sunrises, as well as nearly as many of waterfalls and mountain scenery. Amaroso had, apparently, a lot of talent with the pictures. About thirty of them were of women standing by what was probably the tower wall, with the sunset colors behind. They were effective, and very well-composed. A large section of the wall behind the desk had the pictures displayed.

"Well, there was no note at the tower. There isn't one here. Eighty nine percent of suicides leave notes," Naldo said. "If there had been a camera with him, I'd close it right down as accidental, but it doesn't seem right. He knew that tower. There are hundreds of pictures here, taken from it over a period of at least two years.

"The sunrise this morning was one he would definitely have wanted. A large rounded cloud formation over the mountains, with a few small clouds above. All salmon, flamingo, and gold.

"I watch the sunrises. It's as I get to the station, and I'm heading east, so I'm going right toward it. You can't help but notice it, unless you're blind.

"It's mostly a feeling. I've seen twenty or thirty suicides before. I know damned well this wasn't one. At night, maybe. In the morning, with that sunrise, which he would appreciate more than most, the psychology of a bright new day? No way!

"It could have been accidental, but he was on the east side of the tower. The rail was at waist height to him. He would have to have been sitting on it. He wouldn't have gone over unless he was. He landed on his back, so he didn't climb onto the rail and fall off that way. His back was to the east, there. If he was on the rail, facing east, he would have hit front first.

"That sunrise, and he was sitting there with his back to it?

"No damned way in hell!"

"So he wasn't there to take pictures. A lot here have some woman sitting on the rail, with the sunrise behind," Maria considered. "Naldo, he was sitting on that rail. Very definitely, and most certainly, or whatever else, he was sitting on that rail – with his back to the sunrise.

"That means someone was there."

"Yes. Someone was taking his picture. If he accidentally fell off that rail, she would report it, immediately, loudly, and hysterically.

"Nobody reported it. He was sitting there, and was pushed over. It was fifty-fifty he would yell and be heard.

"Maria, she has the camera. If it was his, and we can find it, it will tag her."

"You're sure it was a woman?"

"There's no picture from there with a man in it. There are pictures of more than thirty women, but no men, at the tower."

Maria agreed that was probably the way it went. "We have to find which woman wanted him dead. We have quite a selection here, so maybe we can narrow it down and find her."

"I don't think the killer's picture will be here, Maria. Look at these. No two are of the same woman.

"He probably took several of each one, and kept the best. I think this is his scoreboard."

Maria studied the wall for a moment. She turned over a picture, to find a name and date on the back. There was only a date on the ones without women in them.

"I see. He laid them and took their picture up there, like the old notch on the headboard. He was a rich, handsome man. He wouldn't carve a notch on his fancy headboard. The damned thing probably cost him ten thousand dollars. He didn't mark up his property, if this room and the front entrance are any indication.

"I recognize a couple of these women. They're high-society, for the most part. One or two are just exceptionally pretty.

"I'm making a psychological profile of him in my mind. He probably didn't get much pleasure out of the society queens. The pretty local girls, he probably did.

"Naldo, he was probably competing with someone in some sick kind of game, like the computer things. These were his conquests, his hits.

"Those games, you're always at risk of getting hit, yourself."

"He wouldn't take the chance that the hit could be fatal."

"Maybe someone else did."

Naldo nodded. "I still think we're looking for a woman."

"I do, too. It's a possibility we have to consider, with this kind of thing. Whether it was a woman who actually did it, there will be one behind it."

They collected all the pictures with people in them, and were moving to search the desk when Mrs. Carter came to ask what they thought they were doing. Naldo explained that there was a question or two about the death. She would get a receipt for anything they took as evidence. It would all be returned, when and if it was not important to the case.

The desk yielded nothing except a very thick address book. It was all women, some names that were very familiar, and some that were not. There was another address book. It was smaller, and pocket-sized. It listed businesses and male names.

"He was one sick bastard," Maria said. "He actually has stars by several of these women. I wonder if any of them were proud to have earned a star from him. There are a couple with two stars! What a wild *thrill*!" She flipped through. "There's one with three stars. I wonder if she got some kind of special prize, like he would sleep with her again."

They didn't find anything more. There was a ledger with his bank balances (he had money in four banks) that showed he had more than six million dollars in cash. It was legitimate. Not from laundering.

"Well, might as well get back. There's nothing here we can do, unless we get a definite bit of evidence," Naldo announced, a few minutes later. "He was neat enough that we can see what there is to see without having to decode his system."

Maria agreed. They gave Mrs. Carter the receipt, and headed back to the station. This case was going to be difficult to impossible. There were far too many possible suspects. The system he used made it probable that the killer wasn't among those photos or in the address book.

Both Maria and Naldo had come to the solid

conclusion that this was murder. One factor told them that: His back had been to the sunrise colors when he went over that rail. That said it all – and nothing. It told them someone was there, taking his picture, with the spectacular sunrise as background. It didn't give a hint as to who.

Well, a hint. She wasn't in the pictures they had. None of those had been on that tower twice.

"That we know of," Maria mumbled. "He didn't take their picture up there twice."

Maria suddenly cried, "Naldo! Look! There's an internet website in the address book that doesn't have a name connected, except 'Me!' I wonder if that crud posted his scoreboard on the web! I wonder if the pictures are the ones on that wall!"

Naldo turned his desk computer around and connected to the web. He asked for the website.

campeondedavid1_1st@aaamy.net

It was a very fancy, well-constructed site that featured photos of sunsets. Regardless of other considerations, Naldo had to admit Amarosa had been a superb photographer.

Page one had two hundred shots taken from Boca Chica. Most featured the sunset on the horizon across the Pacific. They were achingly beautiful. Cloud formations that had features like animal shapes or faces were among the most effective. There were notations about the pictures under each photograph. Two said the pictures were enhanced, but not altered, to bring out the features.

"He was totally honest about that. It shows he was as good a photographer as I thought." Naldo said.

Page two was from David, from the tower, to the greatest degree. They were as good and as well-presented. There were no people in them.

Page three was waterfalls and rivers.

Page four was mountain scenes,

Page five was scenes from and across the ocean, some were on the Caribbean side, and some on the Pacific.

Page six was titled: *People I have Known and Sunset Blend*. It was the pictures on the wall, plus pictures from Boca Chica Island, with women backgrounded by a sunset.

Naldo studied the pictures. None of the women were the same ones as in David.

"Total of seventy six women. Quite the stud, I'd say," Maria said, sourly. "Naldo, I'd say this is his official scoreboard."

"I think so. We can be ninety five percent or more certain the killer's picture isn't here."

"I've been thinking. We simply have to find the camera. The killer's picture will be on it – and his picture will be on it."

"We can hope, but it will be deleted."

"Naldo! Go back to his homepage!"

Naldo shrugged, and went back.

"Let's try those. You can click directly," Maria said, pointing to the *other sites of interest* near the bottom. There were four.

gooodbyirenefifty4 was a site that featured a blog and pictures of paintings by a woman named Irene Goodly. She had died recently, and her sister kept the blog going. The paintings were portraits. Amarosa was one of them. They were lifelike and good.

buddymybuddychal50plus was another photo site. They weren't half as good as Amarosa, but it was plain, knowing what they felt they knew, this was another "competitor." It didn't have the pages of other photos. It was photos of women, mostly taken by a fancy swimming pool.

Maria studied the photos. "Several the same as Amarosa. Only fifty two. A puny amateur!"

newgirlontheblock2013 was a number of photos of various things on page one.

Page two had only two pictures. They were of the old tower, from a distance. The sunrise told Naldo they were taken that morning.

There seemed to be two people on the tower observation walk, in the first one. The sunset was behind.

The second had only one person on the walk.

They were thumbnails, so Naldo brought up the photo by clicking on it. There were definitely two people on the walk. A man and a woman. The man was wearing the same type of clothing Amarosa was wearing when he took the dive. The woman had on a white blouse, and was wearing a skirt.

The photo was dated and timed in the data box. It really was taken that morning, at 6:04AM.

"Naldo! Do you know what this is!?" Maria exclaimed.

"It's a picture of Amarosa and a woman, taken this morning, of a distance shot of the tower. It was within minutes of when he died."

He expanded the second photo. It was just the woman, looking over the rail. There was a faint figure of a man, falling from the tower.

"We have it!" Maria cried. "We have the killer's picture! Zoom it!"

Naldo was shaking a bit as he expanded the picture. He was looking at the photograph of a murder!

"Oh, holy shit! Damn it to hell!" Maria cried.

The picture pixelated long before it brought out any features of the woman. It was from too far, and was with a lower resolution.

Naldo checked the data box. Resolution of the original photo was just 2.1 megapixels. The distance meant it wouldn't be possible to enhance it to bring out any features.

"Well, we can show it was murder, and that a woman killed him," Naldo said, tiredly.

"What was the time on the second?"

"So. We can show a woman was there. She would have to be part of it, but there could have been someone else," Naldo said.

"Like I said, 'Holy shit, and damn it to hell!'"

Naldo shook his head. "We have to get in touch with the women in those pictures. We can match the names to the address book. It should be easy enough to contact most of them.

"Maria, it will be to you to interview them. This is about sex, so a man won't get half the answers a woman would."

Maria nodded. "We might as well get started. I'd suggest starting with now, and working backward. It's more likely it's a recent one.

"I don't know if a phone interview will work. I have to see their faces.

"Naldo, there was a name on the desk. That slip of paper. It said La Tipica, Sylvia M. Slum.

"Adding it up, the man and woman on the tower were not in fancy clothes. It was normal kinds of things. It would be what the upper crust people considered slumming clothes. He was as upper crust as they come, and Sylvia M. could be Sylvia Morales. She's a beauty, she's not in those pictures, she's richer than Midas.

"You can see what I mean. Anyone who would consider La Tipica slumming? Gimme a break!"

Naldo went through the address book. Sylvia Morales was the newest entry in the M section.

Maria called, and was put through to Sylvia, after a few minutes.

"Hi. Police? I just got up. A bunch of us went to that new disco last night, and got snozzled. I'm just trying to get my head together.

"Police? What did we do this time?"

"I'm calling about Armando Amarosa. You were with him last night?"

"We started with him, but dumped him at that Frog place."

"'We' who? It's important. You started at La Tipica?"

"Yes. It was a setup to take the ... what's going on? What has Army done that you got involved because of?

"My head is splitting. Don't drink tequila all night long and expect to feel anything better than purely horrible the next day."

"I'm afraid Mr. Amarosa is dead. Murdered."

There was a long shocked silence, then, "Army is dead? Who would kill him? He was pathetic. You'd like to do ... what we did.

"Maybe someone he had used did something, but kill?

"It's possible someone got mad enough to hit him with a bottle or stick him with a knife, but kill?"

"Can you tell me a little about last night, who was there, and what happened? You say you dumped him at the disco? 'We' indicates that more than one was involved in, you said, setting him up? How? Why?"

"Officer, maybe I can get a liter of coffee in me and can meet you somewhere? It would take a long time, and the telephone isn't the best form of communication."

"Thank you. I'm Maria. Maria Lanias.

"Miss Morales, this case seems, somehow, to be connected with sex. It appears Amarosa was a predator. I'm working on the case with a male officer. Would it be asking too much for him to be there to add his experience?"

"No. I'm not known to be shy about that kind of thing. None of us are.

"The police station. This started, so far as I'm concerned, with La Tipica. That's a block from the station. An hour and a half?"

"Thank you, Miss Morales. We appreciate your help. We don't often get any from ... sorry."

"From the snob crowd, who will have you off the force in a heartbeat, if you don't back off?

"I'm Syl. I'll be there. Maybe I can call a couple of the others who were there, and we can come up with something. It's sort of exciting. Not good exciting, but you couldn't believe how boring this life can be. Half the time, I envy the comon working person, who has a purpose in existing."

"I like you, Syl! I'm Maria."

"She do it?" Naldo asked, when she hung up.

"I doubt it. I'd still like her, if she did!"

"Well, it will be about time for some food. Let's get the records up to date and go to a meeting!

"I wonder. Who else will be there?"

"Whoever, I think it will be interesting. I hope they're real people, like Syl, and not a bunch of those self-important rich snobs."

They got the file in proper order, listed the things for the evidence vault, then headed for La Tipica. It had a number of people there for their late lunch. There was room at a side table, then Maria suggested one of the long tables out front.

They had just finished the meal when a Rolls Royce stopped to the side, and a woman wearing thousands of dollars worth of jewels got out, followed by Sylvia, then by another woman, who was dressed far less expensively. They stood, looking around, so Maria went to invite them to the table. Sandy Bellows and Essy Generoso were introduced by Sylvia Morales.

Naldo couldn't help noticing that, while these women were obviously wealthy, they were also naturally beautiful. It wasn't makeup.

"I'm afraid I'm an ostentatious show-off sort, but you'll find I can be human," Sandy said. "I wouldn't come here for much of anything else, but Syl says Army is dead? Murdered?"

"Yes. He was shoved or thrown off of the old church tower this morning," Maria answered. "All of you, except Sylvia, have pictures taken there at sunset or sunrise."

"We found out about his website. His score card," Sandy said. "It was part of what we were doing last night. We all just happened to come here when he was here with who he thought would be the next picture. We got together and decided to humiliate him, in public, the way he tried to humiliate us.

"No one here is a virgin, or pretends to be. We didn't care about the site, except that it was a cheap and sneaky thing to do.

"What we did was come here like we were all on the way to the new disco, and just happened to see him and Syl, so we stopped and acted like it was pure chance we were going to the place. We all made statements that others could overhear about the men in our crowd not quite making the grade, 'Oh, sorry, Army!' but maybe there was a man who could handle a woman at the disco.

"We had a woman he knew call him while we were here and ask him to meet her. We made it to where he couldn't accept, but he would see her tomorrow.

"We climbed into my car and went to the disco, where we all ogled the other men and as much as ignored him. There was a friend he had tried to get to, there. She's a rather mousy type, but is a good person. She doesn't play the games we play. She called him, and they left. She would give him the old, 'Not on the first date! Tomorrow would be the second date, wink wink,' bit.

"Everyone there had noticed that there was this goodlooking dude sitting at a table with several reasonably attractive women, but they treated him like a brother, if that. It would make them think he was gay. If he hadn't left when he did, I would have pointed out some handsome man to him and say he was a dream, didn't he agree? Essy would say she knew one, who she really did, and that he was gay, but a really nice guy. Did Army want to meet him?

"We were going to show him how it feels to be treated like a number on a scorecard. Gloria, that's Gloria Sanchez, was dressed like a Latina sexpot, with a red Tango dress split skirt that was so tight it cut off the circulation. She was going to say, a little too loud, that she always had more fun with a gay man. They knew how to treat a woman. Army would know about that.

"We can be a vicious, malicious bunch of bitches, when provoked!"

"We just wanted to watch him squirm and stop him from doing anything about what it would do to his reputation. He and that Tommy Gaines character have some kind of bet, I think. If it's true about the other websites, we would work it on all of them!" Essy said. "Here's Mandy. She likes the slumming scene, and knew a lot of people at the disco, so we were able to do a real job on Army."

Another attractive woman came from a taxi to the table to be introduced as Mandy Winters. She was dressed more like the other people in the place. Clean and neat and attractive, but not expensive.

"We were telling them about our little play with Army," Sylvia said. "I guess you know he's dead."

"I just heard it on the radio. You said to meet you here with the police, so I can figure it.

"How much do they know, so far?"

"They know he was murdered, about how he was, about what we did last night, about the website," Sylvia answered.

"Murdered? They just said he fell from that tower where he took all of us to get a picture for his stupid scoreboard," she replied. "He was murdered? This morning? One or more of us did it?"

She laughed, and called for the waitress to bring them a large sizzle platter. Shrimp al ajillo.

"Probably one of your crowd, but not the ones here," Maria said. "I've had monster hangovers, so can tell by looking at you that you all have. You weren't up at a quarter to six to kill him."

"I don't think it was one of our crowd. Not because of the kinds of things he did to us. We would just do what we did. Get even, in the same coin," Sandy said. "I called Gloria. She says she can come over. She won't have a hangover. She doesn't drink more than one drink a night. Her mother was alcoholic, and she isn't going to let that happen to her.

"Donna won't come. She was part of it. She called him while we were here to goad him into having the spine to tell us to go to hell and going with her. It didn't work, but I saw Clara Enders at the disco, and set him up with her. All promises. She doesn't sleep around, like we do.

"Well, we don't get much sleep!"

Naldo laughed, and said it was refreshing to meet people who didn't deny they were human. He didn't sleep around very much, but it wasn't because he didn't try!

"Honey, you're nice enough looking, and the

kind of guy who won't play stupid games, so be careful! We're a horny lot! You might end up sleeping around a lot more!" Mandy said.

"Oh, that would be just *awful*!" Naldo shot back. "I'm *not* that kind of ... guy!"

"You, I like," Essy shot at him. "I'll bet you're good in bed. You don't think you're the world's hottest superstud. That kind are always a big disappointment."

"Army's not here. We don't need to keep the act going," Sylvia said.

"What act?" Essy asked, with all innocence. Sylvia gave her the bird.

The sizzling platter of excellent shrimp with garlic came, along with rice and French fries and onion rings and salad. They joked, and had fun during the meal. Naldo had enough to eat, already, as did Maria, but they insisted it was too much without the two joining them. They decided they didn't want Army dead, but it wasn't a big deal that he was.

Maria managed to get three names of people who might have been in league with Amarosa on the sex scoreboard deal.

Gloria Sanchez came during the meal. She was certainly what Naldo would call a hot number. She was sexy as hell, and played to it. She was fun, too. Naldo liked all these people. He hadn't thought he would.

They went back to the station to put what they found together. While it had been a fun time, and he had met people he could like and relate to, he was a cop. So was Maria. They were on a case. They would do what they could to solve it. That was never a secret with the people at that table. They respected him for being open about it.

Now to do the dribble-sift thing. Sift through hours of reading and investigating for the dribble of important information. That was always a big part of this kind of police work. As the old novels used to say, "It's legwork time."

First order of business: check out those three names. Find out where all the women in those pictures were now.

Naldo would take the three names, while Maria would check on the pictures.

Naldo looked at the note. It was just three names that didn't mean much. Tommy Gaines, Arturo Veras, Samuel LaPerla.

He sighed, and went to the computer for a search, which showed they were just wealthy younger landowners who didn't make much of a splash. Gaines had published some things on blogs, which led to finding reference websites, one of which they had already seen. He was *buddymybuddyfiftyfour.*

Arturo Veras was the oldest. 34. He was quiet, and was thought to be "connected" to money laundering, but investigation left him clean. It was more the people he associated with.

Samuel LaPerla was, very likely, gay. Naldo felt that one would definitely not be any part of this kind of sex scheme.

Maybe he was, but with men? Maybe Amarosa was his picture on a website, assuming LaPerla had one.

Then it would be the other way around. LaPerla would be the victim.

Why was he mentioned in a discussion of sex scoreboard types?

"Maria, who mentioned this Samuel LaPerla character as a possible member of the sex scoreboard thing?"

Maria had excellent recall. "Mandy. It wasn't directly about the scoreboard. She said it ... Syl and Essy were talking about something, then. A woman who was on the scoreboards, and Mandy said something about it. I connected it to him having a scoreboard, but that may not be. Why?"

"He's gay. He wouldn't be likely to have that kind of scoreboard."

"Oh."

Naldo thought about it, then looked up Mandy's number and called.

Naldo asked Mandy why she connected Samuel LaPerla to Amarosa's website, or did she mean LaPerla had a website of the type.

"Sammy's gay. I think he has a website, but it's not that kind of thing. His little sister was on Army's scoreboard, or something. Sammy was pissed. I put it to his sister playing the sweet chaste maiden, and he was mostly pissed because the illusion was shattered. I can give you his number, but he's in Costa Rica, I think. Maybe I can find Ana's number. She'll still be here.

"To be honest with you about it, I think she's been screwing someone for years! Her act of a little sexpot is too good to not be based on experience.

"Ah! Ana LaPerla Salvina. Eight six four five nine ninc two seven. Don't tell her where you got it."

"You had it right there?"

"What? Oh! It's on the electronic book thing. I punch 'L' and it brings up all of those, then I punch 'ap'. It's the only one that starts with 'Lap' and there are just the two. Ana and Sammy."

"LaPerla de Salvina?"

"No. She's not married. It was her mother's name."

"Thanks, Mandy."

"Want a fast romp? See if you're as good as I'd think you'd be?"

"Never on the first date! Tomorrow would be the second date, wink, wink."

"You're fun. Somehow, I always thought a cop wouldn't be."

"I always though a rich woman would be a royal pain in the ass. Maybe we were both wrong."

"You're good! That line would definitely work if I was with you at the disco!"

They teased a minute, then Naldo sat back. He really was surprised that those rich – he almost thought "bitches" – would be such regular, good people. These certainly were!

"Maria, did you come across an Ana LaPerla or Ana Salvina in those pictures?"

LaPerla ... no. Salvina ... yes. Here it is. She rifled through the ones she had already listed, and handed him a picture of a pretty girl. She looked like she was about fifteen or sixteen years old!

"Maria? Are there very many of those girls this young in that mess?"

"She just looks young, I think. He would be a fool to put anyone underage on that site."

Naldo went to the computer and looked up the name to see if she had a cedula. She did. It was issued just two months ago. She was seventeen.

"When was the picture taken? What's the date on it?"

"September three, twenty twelve."

"She was underage by two months. I think I want to talk with her!" He called the number Mandy had given him. It was a private cell phone number.

"Yes?"

"Ana LaPerla? I'm Renaldo Flores, National Police. May I ask you a few questions?"

"Police? Questions? What?"

"Did you know an Armando Amarosa?"

"The one who jumped off the church? I'd met him, I'm sorry to say."

"There's a picture of you on the tower in his home. We have to contact all who were ever there with him."

There was a silence. He went on. "We seem to have to come to the conclusion that those pictures are all of his ... conquests."

"Okay."

"You were underage by three months when that picture was taken."

"I won't bring charges. It wouldn't prove any-thing. I was stupid, so have to live with it."

"It was with consent?"

"Depends on what you call 'consent,' doesn't it?"

"It wasn't rape. That's all I want to know."

"Depends on what you call 'rape,' doesn't it?"

"I don't know. That's why I'm asking."

"It wasn't by consent, but I put myself in the situation, okay? I just wish it wasn't impossible to just forget it! The first time's supposed to be special, not just specially horrible!

"I'm glad he's dead! So there!" She hung up.

Maria had heard his end of it. She raised an eyebrow.

"He as much as raped her. She was a teenager with ideas of wonders, and it was horrible. She's glad he's dead, so there!"

"Brother got revenge?

"No. You said he's in Costa Rica.."

"He's *supposed* to be in Costa Rica. I have a definite suspect, at last!"

"It's more than I have."

"I'm going to ... I have to know which ones. I wish you could be along. You catch things I miss.

"Maria, I'm going bar-hopping tonight! Gay bars!"

"Like every night? How do you know a gay bar, here? They go to all of them. Nobody gives a damn, and it's no big deal."

"There are a couple where the higher classes go."

"What will you prove?"

"I'll learn if he really is in Costa Rica."

"You don't think he is?"

"Come on! He's my only real suspect!"

"He's your excuse to go bar-hopping. Gay bars, yet!"

He gave her the finger.

"No. You. Don't drop the soap in the shower."

He went home to change into more of the type of clothes for bars, then went out toward Alanje. He'd heard of two places not far from there, and it wasn't far from there where LaPerla had a large estate where he grew sugar cane and rice.

"Hi. I'm here because Sammy LaPerla thinks this is a great place," Naldo announced, to the bartender. "Not many here, huh?"

"It's early. We don't get started until ten thirty or so. What'll you have?"

"Well, a Balboa. I don't want to get wasted before the party starts."

The bartender gave him a Balboa, and went to wait on another man who came in.

He looked around. LaPerla did come there. The bartender didn't ask who Sammy Whatever was.

This was an upscale place. He was sort of sorry he didn't ask what beer cost. He would probably end up paying two or three dollars for a seventy five cent beer.

He saw the sign over the bar. Beer was a dollar, until ten, then was a dollar and a quarter. Fair enough!

There was a man, about twenty, by the jukebox. He asked Naldo what he wanted to hear.

"Oh, Mana, Sin Bandera, Marco Antonio Solis, Vicente Fernandez. I don't like the typical or, especially, regaton. It's just noise!"

"Yeah. I like the more romantic things, myself. Ana Gabriel. Amaia Montero." He punched some numbers, and came to sit next to Naldo. *Mariposa* came on.

"You're new. I'm Rigo. I've seen you around David. Is it true that it doesn't make any difference if you're gay on the police?"

"So long as it doesn't interfere with your job. Same as anything else." That was to let him know he wasn't fooling anybody. They'd seen him, and knew he was a cop.

"Are you on duty?"

"In the sense that I always am on duty, but my shift is over for the day. At five."

"You're obviously not gay. What are you here investigating?"

"A man who fell – or was pushed – off a tower came here, at least once. I'm just trying to find who might have wanted him out of the way."

"That Amarosa character? I wouldn't know him if I saw him. How do you know he was here?"

"Red Maserati. Only one around."

"That really handsome, really rich guy who ... had a loud argument with Sammy about Sammy's sister?"

"That's the one."

"I saw him here, that time. It was the only time. He wouldn't ever be allowed back, no matter how much money he has or how handsome he was. Niko won't put up with some ass who comes in and starts trouble with a regular."

"Yeah. We heard about it. I was hoping Sammy would be here, but I'm too early, I think."

"He comes in about nine, a couple of nights a week. He leaves about eleven. He's rich and handsome, and a very nice person. He doesn't leave alone, most times."

"Well, if Army isn't even allowed in here, he certainly didn't leave with him last night!"

He laughed. "No, he left with Gonzo, last night.

"I think Gonzo would be wild in bed, but I'm a coward, when it comes to those really body-builder types. He's supposed to be a dream, but he can get violent. I've seen it – not here! Niko wouldn't put up with it.

"It was at a little bar in David. The motorcycle crowd goes there. Gonzo was with a guy from around there, and one of the bad-asses started some shit. Gonzo kicked his ass. And his buddy's ass, for good measure.

"Gonzo's strictly from his end of the stick. He likes the gay guys. A lot of men do. Great sex, and nobody owns them or gets pregnant, just to trap them."

They chatted. Naldo liked Rigo, who didn't try to hide anything. Rigo wanted to take him home, but he didn't think he could go for that, so was honest about it. Rigo said that was the way of the world. Some liked rice, some liked potatoes, some liked both.

Naldo went back home to sack out for the night. He would talk with Gonzo, tomorrow. He could find him from the police report where he'd kicked the two big motorcycle bums' asses. He remembered hearing about that incident. Contact information on the report. It was self-defense when the hoods harassed a companion and ended up in the hospital.

"Jorge Perina, better known as Gonzo? I'm Renaldo Flores, cop.

"Can I ask you a few questions?"

"Sure! I might not answer them, but you can always ask!"

Naldo laughed. "It's about Sammy LaPerla."

"I'm no part of anything he might have done."

"It's about why."

"I don't know what, so how would I know why?"

"Him offing Amarosa."

"I don't know that he did, but, if he did, it was because Amarosa knocked up his little sister and wasn't going to take responsibility for it."

"He wouldn't have any choice. She was only seventeen."

"When you have as much money as he did, he had a choice."

Naldo nodded. That was much too true, here.

"Who took the pictures?"

"As far as I know, he took them. That's why Sammy found out who it was that knocked up little sister baby. I figured she already knew about everything there was to know, the way she acted, and the way she would be all coy and cute when a guy was around.

"He said she told him everything. She was a virgin when shithead seduced her – which wasn't quite tame enough to be called seduction.

"If she hadn't gotten knocked up, he would have gotten over it, in a couple of months. She did invite it. He was just pissed because he wouldn't do the right thing and marry her until she had the kid, then he could divorce her. It could all be on paper, and was for the kid, not them. She didn't ever want to be in the same world with him again."

"I see. I meant the pictures of Amarosa on that tower with a woman, and him going over the side in the next picture. We have the pictures from the web."

"A woman? Then it wasn't Sammy? You mean you actually have pictures of the dive?"

Naldo gave him the web address. He started to say something, then said he would damned well look up that one!

Naldo went back to the station to report to Maria on everything he'd done, and to file the official report. He felt he knew what happened, now. He wondered if he should act on it.

Maria asked him why the deep thought?

"I have this one figured, all the way. I can't say it wasn't justified, but it could lead to someone thinking the best way to solve a personal problem is to kill someone.

"I want to talk with a couple of people. Maybe I can decide. I can take into consideration how corrupt the court system is here in Chiriqui."

"I see. You do your job, the court throws it out. Everyone gets more or less what they want.

"That's what you mean? No matter what, he'll be watched for the rest of his life. Maybe this was justified. You did your job. After all, we're only supposed to solve cases, not prosecute them."

"Well, you want to come?"

"Wouldn't miss it!"

"Ana? I'm Naldo, the cop who called you. This is Maria.

"Is Sammy here?"

"Yeah. He came back from Costa Rica this morning."

"We have to talk. Is Gonzo here, too?"

"Yeah. He came over. He said for me to be nice when you come. He and Sammy want to talk to you. Come on in."

She led them to a pleasant patio, where Gonzo and a man were sitting at a marble table. Naldo greeted them, and introduced Maria. She said she would go to her room. Naldo asked that she stay.

"I don't have anything to say or to do with anything!"

"You took the pictures on the web. You knew what was going down. Please. It won't make it any worse."

"Stay, Annie," Sammy said. "Naldo and Maria. What deal can we make?"

"None," Naldo replied. "We're the wrong ones. The reports are already filed. You can handle it with the judge. I just want to know a few things for personal reasons.

"To tell the truth, I think it was justified, but you should have walked up to him on the street and blown his brains out.

"Lay it out?"

"He took Ana for a ride in the Maserati. He stopped at a place up past Anastasia. He as much as raped her. She says she asked for it. She had almost promised him, but she changed her mind because he was acting like a pig to her, like he could tell her what to do, and she had to do it.

"I can see her point. She always did act sexy and coy around guys. She put herself in a position she wanted to see what the real thing was like. It couldn't be anything short of heaven. He made it hell for her.

"I would have gotten over it, but she's pregnant, as you can see. All I asked was that he get a paper wedding until the kid's born, then he could divorce her, and the kid would have a mother and father in the church.

"I can see you were going to suggest abortion. We are Catholic, and could never do that.

"We could have worked something with her marrying somebody else, and we could have worked it out, then he put that picture on what he called his scoreboard. It was on the internet, and anyone could see it.

"The women on that scoreboard know about it, and don't care, really. They think he's a snake and a crud, but they aren't pregnant, and are experienced enough that he couldn't use his lines unless they wanted it that way. Several have told me he was a big letdown in the bedroom.

"I was with Gloria Sanchez, teaching her a few things about using makeup – which she doesn't need. Syl called, and told her about what they planned with him. They were going to humiliate him the way he thought he could humiliate them.

"I made a plan, and went to Costa Rica. I went in through Frontera and up to Rio Sereno and walked back.

"Amarosa didn't really like women, officers. It was the scoreboard thing.

"Anyhow, I saw a great opportunity! He would be desperate to get away from his tormentors at the disco and, because of the way they would be treating him, he could get up and walk out at the least opportunity.

"If it had been me, I would have walked out at La Tipica, but it wasn't me.

"I was with a woman who thought he was a sick thing. She would do what I asked, so I arranged for her to be sitting in the disco to wait for an opportunity to call him, suggesting a way for him to escape. It worked. She would tell him she didn't sleep with a man on the first date – but there was tomorrow!

"I could count on him wanting to take her to the tower for photos. He would choose the morning, the sunrise, because afternoons lately have been rainy.

"He did exactly as predicted. He said he would meet her at the church so they could watch a romantic sunrise from the tower to celebrate their new friendship.

"He came to the church at five thirty. I was on the tower, in drag. He saw me up there from below, and came up.

"Did you know he has a key? That's why he can take those pictures there when no one is about. He gave Clara a copy so she could meet him there.

"He came up. I do look good in drag, and it wasn't light enough for him to see I wasn't a woman. I said I was waiting for a friend who had been there once before for the sunrise.

"The colors started, and the light was getting better. I said my friend was going to miss it!

"I talked him into letting me take a couple of pictures with his camera. I said he was a very handsome man, and would he sit on the rail with the sunrise behind him so I could get a picture? He could send it to me on the internet, through my e-mail.

"By then, he knew Clara wasn't coming. I was a woman. He needed something for his scoreboard. This would work out very well for both of us!

"I got the camera, and he sat on the rail. I took one picture, then asked him to give me more of a profile. It was perfect! It was beautiful!

"He turned a bit to his left, to where I could get the profile. I yanked off the wig and shoved. He went over. I went back to Rio Sereno and into Costa Rica, then came home this morning.

"That's about all there is to it."

"Except that you had little sister take pictures of it to put on the web. The resolution wasn't fine enough to be able to say it wasn't a woman up there."

"So that's why she did it! Gonzo told me about the pictures, and we looked at them! It's true! No one could say it was me in drag, not a woman! I was stupid to make this confession.

"Ana, why didn't you tell me?"

"I wanted you to, uh, to really be surprised, you know, about the pictures. You can't lie very well, and I, uh, thought you would be more, you know, like, believable, if you were actually surprised."

"Not to mention the fact that old camera you used wouldn't be able to zoom without pixelating to where you couldn't see it was Sammy," Maria said. "You don't fool me for one second, Honey.

What were you going to do? Blackmail your brother?"

Ana looked defiant, then her eyes flicked around like a trapped animal. She actually hissed.

"Ana?" Sammy asked. "Is it true?"

"I hate you! You ruined my life! You made me go with that piece of shit for my first time! I hate all of you!"

"I made you go with him? What are ... I didn't make...!"

"Nobody but your snobby friends were good enough. I couldn't go with anybody I wanted! You forced me to go with him! I blame you! I hate you!

"Why couldn't it have been Gonzo? He's what I needed, but I ended up with that egomaniac bastard and got pregnant! You won't even let me get rid of his brat! I hate you! I hate him! I hate this brat growing inside of me!

"I want to die!" She ran into the house.

"How dramatic!" Maria said. "That should take the Emmy, or Grammy, or whatever for the worst performance of the year!

"Come on, Naldo. Sammy can take care of that psychopathic piece of work, himself."

"Officers, what should I do? I had no idea! She was trying to ... she wanted those pictures to show that it was me?"

"Lord! You haven't seen that she's as looney as a Toucan?" Maria answered. "Lord! Give me strength! This isn't the first time she's come at you with that crap!"

"I thought she was just distraught because of what happened," he replied.

"Check the DNA of the kid. I'll bet even money it isn't Amarosa's," Maria said. "Everyone who's known her says she's always acting the sex kitten, and is coy around men. She's sexually active when she does that at that early age. She started it when she was twelve or thirteen, right?"

"I guess ... yes. Maybe just twelve," Sammy replied.

"So she was molested when she was eight or nine. I doubt you could have done anything, but it might have been not so bad if you'd known. It's your problem. I do think you should get that DNA test. She can't play you with the sweet little virgin, then."

"She's only with me because my brother is a lowlife. She wanted to go with him, but I stopped it.

"He would be the one who started what ended up as this?"

"There's a good chance."

"She can't be changed, can she?"

"I very seriously doubt it."

"Then she goes to Bert's. I'm through trying with her. I killed a man because of her, and she was going to use that to blackmail me. Any obligation I ever had is over and done!"

Naldo and Maria went back to the station. They both had to get away from that lovely domestic scene.

"I think I'm so glad I ain't rich I don't know what to do!" Maria said.

"Syl and Mandy and Essy and Gloria are rich. Not many are like them.

"And they all say life is boring, if you have too much."

"I can see how that would be. Still, I'd like to give it a try!"

"How are we going to report this?"

"As I told Sammy, the reports are already filed. All we do is say we have confirmed the evidence. It's somebody else's problem."

Naldo read the official report by the court. Insufficient evidence. Case dismissed with full recourse to refiling should further evidence be presented.

"There won't be further evidence," Maria said.

"Even if there is," Naldo agreed. "I heard from Gonzo. He said Sammy sent his dear sister to his brother, in Panama' City. She's happy with that. It seems the baby was miscarried. He had a DNA test done, discretely. It wasn't Amorosa's, as expected."

"Well, it was really justifiable homicide, from Sammy's perspective. He really thought he was doing the right thing.

"Ana's causing brother Bert problems. He's the type who'll put her on the streets."

"She'll arrange for him to get killed, if he does.

"Well, we can get on to the next case. This one was as much as dismissed. Sammy has too much money for anything else."

"I don't know. I like some of those rich people. I think Mandy really does want me to date her. I'm the exotic low-class cop, and she's the heiress who falls in love with an idea."

"She's not about to fall in love! It's all sex! You men are so stupid! All that'll happen is you get laid by some rich beautiful woman! That's all that'll happen!"

"As expected," Naldo replied, smugly.

That got him the finger.

C. D. Moulton's works are available on most major outlets as printed or e-books. CD writes the CD Grimes, PI mysteries, the Det. Lt. Nick Storie mysteries, the Clint Faraday mysteries, the Flight of the Maita science fiction series, books on orchid culture and many others of many types. Mystery, adventure, intrigue, science fiction, fantasy, para-normal, mild erotica, and factual.